Who Stole My
$15,000,000
Mansion?

'Country' Nate Green

authorHOUSE®

AuthorHouse™
1663 Liberty Drive
Bloomington, IN 47403
www.authorhouse.com
Phone: 1 (800) 839-8640

Published by AuthorHouse 08/18/2016

ISBN: 978-1-5246-2548-1 (sc)
ISBN: 978-1-5246-2547-4 (e)

Print information available on the last page.

This book is printed on acid-free paper.

Scripture quotations marked KJV are from the Holy Bible, King James Version (Authorized Version). First published in 1611. Quoted from the KJV Classic Reference Bible, Copyright © 1983 by The Zondervan Corporation.

Conference

Office...Shays Barker a dedicated young 36 yr. old who has been working diligently for Auturo-Engineering and construction for no less than 10 years. The manager owner Levi Burlingame has set a meeting to name a brand new Regional Vice President. The opening comes about as a result of their present Vice President who is leaving because he has been offered a lucrative contract in show business. Shays, who has superior potentials in the field, yet has been passed up on two occasions. In spite of his major contributions to the company above and beyond the call of duty. Mr. Levi Burlingame, the owner and President, has seen fit to offer Shays various "reasons" to pass him up. There is a great deal of wonderment questions and anticipation in this breath taking, heart palpitating, and scenario. Employees are talking and sipping their drinks as they await the biggest decisions the company has had to make in five years, as they drink and make inquiring comments. Mr. Burlingame rises from his seat looks over is crowd of workers-taps against a glass louder and louder. He calls for everyone to quiet down. He begins to give an elaborate talk on the high-lights of the company. He gives honors to at least 3 of his departmental heads and then calls Shays Barker's. Shays comes through the crowd from the back of the room and stands facing Mr. Burlingame with a smile. Burlingame expresses in a pompous way, he and the company are eternally grateful for Shays loyalty and contributions but he is going to follow the dictates of his mind. He introduces a man who is a friend with considerable influences his company needs and he is accepting the bid of Craig Miller as Vice President for Auturo-Engieering and Construction. Shays smile turns and expression of sheer disbelief, as he screams NO NO NO...

He continues to scream how Burlingame used him naming what he has done to promote the company and how much this position meant to him and Mr. Burlingame tries to offer consolation to Shays, but to no avail, Shays is so distraught that he calls Burlingame all kinds of names like liar and low-life. Shays last blasting words are-you'll pay for this Burlingame. As God is my witness, you will pay and pay dearly!!! The crowd gives off its ooh and aaah, as Shays turns and storms out through the stunned crowd.

One Month Later

Time has passed – Shays has given much
thought to his plan of vengeance.

Having arrive in a highly secured and most exclusive area;
Shays views the entire scene with anticipation. As his eyes scan
the well – designed homes, one can only conclude that this is truly
an extraordinary panorama. He soon spies a.. home offset some
distance from the rest. This is the home he has come to…his point
of destination.

He walks from his observance point to the front door. There are
beautiful flowers on both sides of the long walkway.

He knocks…. moments go by…. No response. He knocks again,
and again, Shays is seen through a curtain in a high window by a
black African-American man later 60's.

Soon the peephole door opens.

Burger

State your business!

Shays

My name's Shays Barker. I'm the engineer at Auturo-Engineering.
I work for Mr. Burlingame. Burger immediately opens the door-
greeting him. Burger-Shaking Shays hand.

Mr. Shays-Mr. Shays Barker. What joy for me to finally meet
cha. Mr. Burlingame has spoken about you many times. Come in…
Come in!!!

My name is Burton James – I used to eat a lot of Burgers and Fries
till my friends' jus' started callin' me Burger.

Shays's Response

Glad to meet you Burger

Shays enter Burlingame's lavishly furnished exquisitely decorated home with plush sofas and glass coffee tables. The walls are featuring DeVinci Paintings Etching's in Ink. The look of success is all through – out this fantastic home.

Burger

This is quite an occasion for me Mr. Barker; you know Mr. Burlingame has spoken your name many a time. You're a household word.

Shays (taken by surprise)

I'm a household word??

Burger (rein forcing)

Yep! Hardly a day goes by your name ain't mentioned. Wait jus a minute Burger leaves the room. Shays sits for just a moment shaking his head.

Shays

A household word....He rises and begins once again looking at the furnishing on his lavish home. He comes across a picture of Mr. Burlingame and his wife. He picks the picture up... looks at it as a burst of anger rises in him. His total expression has changed... it appears he is going to do something drastic when his mood is interrupted by the voice of Burger holding a small tray & standing in the doorway on the tray a bottle of vintage red wine and 2 glasses.

Burger

I believe they love each other.

Shays (turning to face Burger)

Who?

Burger (moving to shapely table)

Mr. & Mrs. Burlingame. I believe they love each other although..........she's very demanding. Here Mr. Barker lets have a spot of red wine, as they say.

Burger pours the wine into the 2 glasses. Shays places the picture back...and steps to pick one of the glasses off the tray. Burger extends his glass and says. "To a lasting friendship."

Shays (extending his glass)

To a lasting friendship
The glass clicks together as both men swallow the wine

Shays

Aahh (wiping his mouth) mighty fine wine

Burger

Mr. Burlingame always insists in the best here! Let's have another one. Burger pours wine into Shays extended glass and then into his glass.

Burger (clearing his throat)

Hmm Hum! That was better than the first one! Shays just smile and puts his glass on the tray. Burger places his glass on the tray and continues. Mr. & Mrs. Burlingame left yesterday for New York. They took that pretty Rose Royce of theirs. They said they were going to ship from there to England. They expect to be gone... man a long trip. Hope your business with Mr. Burlingame wasn't too important.

Shays (quickly)

No, he mentioned his sewer. Said he wanted me to come out and remove the system, well I've been real busy, thought I'd better get on it before my work load starts up again, understand you can smell the sewer.

Burger

And how!!! Man let me show you! Burger leads the way from the living room to a small corridor, which passes a well, decorated dining room and leads to an immaculate well-kept kitchen. As Burger goes out the rear screen door he warns Shays we've got a couple steps so watch it!

Shays goes through the rear door and steps down to the yard. He looks over a spacious backyard. At both corners of the yard are 2 large monuments. The yard is ever so green up to the long break in the ground from the house to the end of the yard. Shays begins inspecting the open sewer line.

Shays (speaks kneeling at ditch)

Some of Mr. Burlingame's work??

Burger (answering as he pulls his handkerchief from his pocket and puts it over his nose.) Yep-he started this a while back…but you know Mr. Barker, I been working here going on four years (coughing) I've come to stand almost anything…but not his sewer…No indeed not this sewer. He wipes his nose, turns and goes back into the house. Shays takes a handkerchief out of his pocket holds it to his nose, as he proceeds to check the soil with his hands. He reaches his hand once again in his pocket and pull out a tape measure. Moments pass as a series of measurements are made.

Shays returns to the living room wiping his hands on his handkerchief.

Burger (seated)

Now you see what I'm talking about.

Shays

I'd better get an early start on it there's an awful lot of work to be done.

Burger

Mr. Burlingame was right about you. He said if you want to get a job done right get Shays Barker and your worries are over!

Shays (once again surprises)

He said that!! Burlingame said that about me!!!

Burger

Shore's that God's truth, when Mrs. Burlingame wasn't around-him and me talked about his business often times, ya see my wife used to cook for him till she wasn't able anymore. He needed somebody to help out round here... so she told him about me.

Shays

...and how does he treat you???

Burger

Oh fine now. We use to go tit for tat on thangs...but he found out...I have a strong constitution ***change of thought* You remember the Deltarasco Account??

8

Shays

Yes-but that was 3 years ago. You know about that?

Burger

Well I told you we talked. He said that's when he was really
sold on your engineering skills…. Cause that was one of his worst
accounts and you came through for him with flying colors.
Shays (really taken)
I can hardly believe what I'm hearing!

Burger

Ah don't be modest Mr. Barker. You have terrific skills-Mr.
Burlingame said so; he told me (slight whispering) he was going to
make you Vice President of Auturo Engineering.

Shays

Vice President??

Burger

Yep! Said he was going to set a meeting date soon.
Shays stand at this remark and seemingly is taken by it. I don't'
mind saying I'm really impressed by what you've said.
Telephone interruption.
Ring. Burger steps to the corridor where the telephone sits on
a stand. He lifts the receiver. Burlingame residence- (A long Pause)
How bad is it this time? (Another Pause) well you'd better check
back with me. Burger places the receiver on the telephone. He stops for
a moment then bows his head Shays rises to leave-Burger apologies.
My apologies Mr. Barker a bit of bad news….You see I have a
sickly brother that's been taken to the hospital. It appears I might
have to leave.

Shays (shaking Burger hand)

I'm truly sorry-But I've met a tremendous man. Thanks for everything. Both men head toward the front door

Burger opens the door and speaks I'd be willing to bet we are not going to have that sewage smell much longer.

Shays

Remember Burger, an early start tomorrow.

Burger shakes his head in acknowledgment closes the door beyond Shays. Burger stands at the door with a dejected look on his face.

My dear brother Roscoe my good man-are going to make it this time??

First Work Day-Early Morning

Burlingame's Backyard

Shays had brought in his 2 men to assist him Jerry White who is working diligently digging along with Handly, a black man in his late 20's. Handy has a handkerchief tie around is head. He's wearing a tee shirt and blue jeans. Both men are wearing gloves.

Shays is bust as he kneel and look through his eye scope and check the information on the note pad. Both men are breathing heavy as they gasp with every shovel of broken still. Much work is being done as time passes. Through the heavy breathing and gasping Burger interrupts as he comes out the rear door holding a tray full of food.

Burger (placing tray on table)

Hey everybody food and drinks for everybody.

Jerry

Alright Mr. Burger, I'm ready for mine…Handly heads to the table behind Jerry. Jerry and Handly proceed to the their refreshments and munch on their sandwiches as Burger goes over to Shays who is standing in the sewer hole.

Burger

Listen – since there's so much traffic here I'm cutting all timing security – the police patrol would be running in all day long. I'll just let them know you're here.

Burger this time uses a hand towel to cover his nose as he turns to go back in the house. Just as he opens the door to step in a voice from behind hollers to him.

Handly (with expression)

Brotherman-hey brother man can ya...Play some music jams for us???

Shays

It'll help Mr. Burlingame's flowerbed. Handly shakes his head-gets a slice of pie and leaves in a backward moonwalk-Micheal Jackson fashion, but trips and falls back through the red door. Handly rolls 2 steps down to the ground. Shays and Jerry rush with food in hand to the door. Handly lays flat on the ground....rolls over and sits up then goes right back into his body rhythm. Shays and Jerry are ecstatic with laughter.

Burger

Soon after a theme of soulful beats and musical rhythms coming across the backyard. Handly with his handkerchief and Burlingame's shirt off revealing his muscular torso brings moves and dances to the heavy sounds.

Saturday: 4 days later shift in music a pretty song play throughout this beautiful home. Burger has a chef's cap on with an apron tie around him in the kitchen. There is a ham in a container as Burger is pouring pineapple juice and putting honey and cloves pineapples are placed on the ham when the cloves and pineapples are placed on the ham when the telephone rings. He goes to a nearby walk phone.

Burger
Burlingame's residence

There is a pause, Burger (shocks) Oh my God…yes I will. He hangs up the telephone, bows his head.

Burger (whispering)

Roscoe-Roscoe, he immediately picks the receiver then the hook and dials a number. Then waits… Burger (very impatient)
Come on come on where are you!!!! He slams the phone to the hook but misses. He then places it correctly he proceeds to call again no response.

Burger (slamming the telephone again)

Where in God's name is everybody???

Burlingame's (backyard)

Moments pass as Burger crashed through the screen, with the screen opening wide a cap on his head and a coat collar turned up music is playing as he interrupts everyone.

Burger (shouting)

Mr. Barker!! Mr. Barker rushed directly to Burger steps down and Shays.

I've got to leave…now! My sister just called from San Francisco said my brother Roscoe just lapsed into a coma….

Shays Interrupts

I'll take charge and contact Burlingame for you…You go…don't' worry.

Burger

I tried to reach his office. I didn't get nobody even tried his private club in England, no luck. I guess I'll try his executive secretary again…couldn't reach her either.

Shays

Leave everything to me Burger I'm sure I'll reach him long before you. Go catch your plane… Burger – (with Reluctance)
I know this is most unusual Mr. Barker most unusual.

Shays

Don't you give another thought. Didn't you say Mr. Burlingame was making me Vice President? The two men walk toward the back porch Burger turns and shakes Shays hand!

Burger

You don't know how much I appreciate this.

Shays

And my very best to your brother Roscoe!

Burger (looks at everyone)

Thanks!!! There's food inside. (he then turns and walks inside)

2 Days Later

In Burlingame's kitchen and 3 men are seated.
Jerry stands to cut some of the remaining portion of ham, as Handly and Shays eat large slices of pie.

Shays speaks

Some kind of meal…Huh fellas?

Jerry

One of the best I've had.

Handly (mouth full)

The brother man really knows how to put it together! Yes!!

Shays

Handly!! Put a few barrels of that dirt on the front flowerbed.

Handly

Oh wow! That…wasteful smelly dirt on the flowerbed? Why.

They continue to work together as Jerry and Shays now apply the new pipes and joints. Handly drives the dump truck to the security point a short way from the house, where he is checked, security also checks the stagnating load. The quaro-holds his nose as he tries to look over but yells to Handly to go on. Handly drives a long distance to a scheduled ravine, backs his truck up to the edge and dumps the entire load over the edge. Handly makes a couple more runs with the truck. The security steps from his security area and sees the truck and the driver-then.

<u>2 more days pass.</u>

The backyard sewer lines have been completed. There is a large pile of waste dirt left. The rest of the lawn is smooth and leveled out.

Jerry

Well it was a helluva job. But we kicked it Shays.

Shays

You guys did such a fantastic job…I'm authorized to give you both a huge bonus.

Handly (Jubilant)

Oww, a bonus?

Shays hands the 2 men envelopes. Both men open their respective envelopes. Sheer joy erupts from both men as they express their gratitude. The two men leave through the rear gate, as Shays heads into the house.

Heavy music interludes –as Shays moves faster than anytime before. He moves to lock the front door-pulls a large bag to the front door. He reaches for the very expensive black paintings on the walls. He wraps them in cellophane and very quickly places them into the bags. There are expensive ornaments wrapped. Drawers are opened where jewelry cases are opened. Diamonds and various jewelry are exposed...then wrapped.

In the master bedroom Shays (angrily voices alone)

So.... You're going to make me Vice-President (Shays walks in front of the mirror near the king size bed).

Shays – (Continuing)

Shays Barker....a household word!! He picks up a near by chair and hunts into the mirror breaking it.

Shays is truly at the height of his anger as he slings cover from the well made bed, he pulls the mattress and throws them down on the floor breathing hard as he stops and looks around- he spies a door across the room he rushes to it. He slings the door open where it exposes a lengthy close of fabulous dress-wear. Silk suits, sporting jackets, topcoats, women suits, over coats, and shoes for the Burlingame galore.

Shays (stand in awe)

My....God will ya look at this!!!!

Shays steps in the closet grapping a huge arm full of racked clothing and throws them on the floor in one great big pile.

After all Burlingame – you can't really blame me. I'm responsible for half of your (breathing very hard) half of your success.

More heavy musical interlude: Shays is seen wrapping the kitchen refrigerator – disconnecting lines. He makes 2 telephone calls: The first he disguises his voice with a handkerchief.

17

Shays (on telephone)

This is the Burlingames' residence. 921 Stouter Drive in Banner Heights. I'm requesting that our water and power be turned off.... yes 30 days (long tunes). Tomorrow? 4 p.m. That'll be fine! Thanks.

Shays (2nd telephone call)

This is Mr. Burlingame at 921 Stouter drives in Banner Heights. We're having a serious sewage problem here- the construction people don't want to hit a gas line, would you turn the gas off temporarily? (Pause), Shays continues to work vigorously placing all wrapped furniture and objects in a central area close to the rear exit. NEXT DAY- The following morning Shays has before him 3 men and 1 woman. A Hispanic family consisting of many construction skills and superior talent. A man and woman around 45 years of age and 2 younger men in their early twenty. They have their construction clothes on, tools on hand ready to work as Shays gives his command.

Shays

Okay! You all have been told what to do. I selected you because I know what you can do. We have just a short time to be here so let's. ....let's move!!!

They scatter to their respective positions as Shays stack his huge truck parked right on the back steps. As Shays step off the trucks. <u>One of the young men steps on loaded down stand assist him</u>. The rotation of loading continues. When the truck is loaded with Burlingame's best to the limit, a tarp cover the entire load over the already wrapped object. After the tarp is secured heavy shovels of messy smelly dirt is put on the secured tarp. The dirt covers the entire truck area. One of the young men gets in the truck and drives from the house and another huge lift truck is backed to the back of the house. Shays continues to stack as much of Burlingame's precious contents on the second truck as much as the truck could hold.

The first truck moves down the road to the area security check. The truck stands as the security man comes out to check, but stops short as it is obvious the odor has reached his nostrils, he reaches for his handkerchief…puts it to his nose…tries to get a quick check but…. motions for the truck to go…as if to say…. please go!!!

The young driver drives a long distance away. He reaches abandon road, turns off the main highway makes it down the road as he looks down a couple of other roads to some obscure location.

He drives through to an area where he sees a fleet of trucks. He has been instructed to leave the truck he has been driving. He backs up and aligns his truck with the rest. His truck is just like the rest as he hops into the cab of one of them and takes off.

Flashes Shays along with the rest of his new crew are working diligently and at record speed to clear the house and load the truck as they leave in rotation of each loaded truck with the tarp secured first, then heavy dirty smelly gunk is spread over the entirety of the truck until the last truck with contents has left. The same procedures works pass the security check and on the second truck exchange.

FULL DAY GONE

All contents and precious belongings of Mr. Burlingame are gone. The home is completely empty other than for Shays and his 4 skillful workers.

(AFTER LOOKING AROUND) Shays speaks

Tomorrow!! The real work begins
Music interlude, then morning—
A large extended tarp is being rolled over the entire home of Burlingame. It takes a few hours to cover the entire roof; the house is now completely covered where a huge sign is put on the front premises that reads

BURLINGAME'S ENTERPRISES HEAVY EXTERMINATION

Removal of the roof is the fist order of business toward the dismantling of the Burlingame's home. Long ladders are brought in as well as chainsaws, ropes dismantling machines that really shorten the span of time to demolish a building. As hammering loosens the beams and using sledgehammers loosens the roof, Shays…the middle age man and his 2 sons work expeditiously against time to complete the first phase of demolition.

The woman is on the floor with a chainsaw in hand, saws the beam in to desired length! Everyone is well hidden under the tarp and cannot be seen from the street nor from the air; because the house is enclosed-like under a tent.

A security car cruises through the neighborhood…two officers check the beautiful homes and landscape.

INTERIOR SECURITY CAR

Officer Marv while is driving speaks
A man couldn't ask for a more beautiful place to live…just look at this scenery… I get a boost just coming up here.

Officer-Ossie speaks

Come on Marv! Step on it (disgustingly) I told you I missed breakfast and my stomach is growlin! Besides, I've seen all this before!
Officer Marv proceeds to accelerate and speed increases where upon he passes Mr. Burlingames' completely <u>tarped-covered</u> home. Officer Marv screeches to a sudden halt.

Officer Marv (shifting in reverse)

What the hell?!

Officer Ossie

You see something!! What is it?

Officer Marv (backing up)

Nobody told me work was going on at Mr. Burlingame!

Officer Ossie (angrily)

Maybe that's because you just got back from your vacation – the Chief was out and I have been on sick leave, here let 's check our chart.
The security car is now parked in front of the tarped home. Ossie checks his chart and after a few moments speaks.

Officers Ossie (elated)

Here it is right here…Burlingame's Extreme Sewage and pipeline under Construction: Both officers pause and take a look at the front scenery.

Officer-Marv

Let's take a look!! (getting out and placing his hat on his head)

Officer Ossie (really disgusted)

Aw for Pete's Sake Marv. We've got it on our computer and our charts!! Officer Ossie gets out reluctantly placing his hat on his head and proceeds behind Marv down the hallway. The flowers on both sides of the walkway have been treated with sewage mud that carries a very stagnant door. As the officers proceed up the walkway they stop, getting the full impact of the door.

Marv-*(reacts) Jeeez –Us ! What is That!!

Marv begins to cough and choke.

Ossie (grabbing his handkerchief)

Well, you wanted to check it out! Backing from around the back is the youngest Hispanic son with a chemical blower that blows fumes. He has proper dress-ware and gear. Fumes, his nose is protected. Whole area of fumes permeate the atmosphere as Corlio continues to back up to the officers.

Water from the sprinkler system has not been turned off and spues over the walkway upon the coughing officers. Officer Ossie tires to avoid the water but accidentally steps off the walkway into the sewage mud flower bed.

Officer Ossie

Oh God! Marv- man lets get the hell out of here!!
Officer Marv ducks and dodges the water but heads back toward the security car wiping his face.

Corlio (turns with a smile speaking Spanish)

More…Spanish is spoken by Corlio as the officers coughing and trying to clear their throats. Ossie's shoes are covered with mud as he tries to knock the mud off.

Officer Ossie (very angry mocking Marv)

Well gees let's check it out- Let's check it out anyway. What was that smell?? And look at my shoes Marv- look at …my shoes!! Both officers get into their security car.

Ossie speaks

Take me to some food Marv! No more stops take me to some food now!!

Marv burns rubber leaving Corlio standing and spitting on Burlingame's front grounds.

Marv –Questions Ossie

You speak Spanish?!

Ossie

Of course I speak Spanish!!

Marv

Well anyway what was he talking about when we left!? What was he saying???

Ossie

He said; I want you two officers to get the hell off my land and get Officer Ossie something to eat!!

Officer Marv (looks questionably at Ossie)

Sure he did_____!!! Both officers laugh and laugh as the security car continues to speed away_____

Corlio (on the lawn) laughs turns and sees Shays beside the tarp_____with thumbs up signal.

Days pass – the roof has been totally removed along with both the rear and side of Burlingame's fabulous home. This leaves the front side and the floors. Shays and Corlio's family work with expert precision as they <u>saw</u> different sections into desired cuts.

The same technique is applied as all cut piles of wood and cement are placed on the every rotating trucks once filled, it is secured and shovels of sewage mud-gunk is put full length of the trucks.

Corlio who does the driving to long distances is assigned to an off beat, yet strategic desert –where dirt was dumped. He backs close to the several hundreds foot drop and dumps the load......

ENTERING LEVI'S BURLINGAME BUILDING

Corridor of Auturo-Engineering the elevator opens-off steps Barker alone. He moves down a winding corridor to where he finally approaches the reception counter. Behind the counter is a tall and very attractive black woman in her mid-20's. She is talking over the telephone when she sees Shays. With the holiday coming up girl! I'm so glad today is Friday!!

Cissy (excusing herself)

Ma! Let me call you back. She looks directly at Shays and speaks-Shays! Where in the world have you been?! Cissy comes from behind the counter confronts Shays and proceeds to embrace him affectionately. Shays responds by kissing Cissy gently on her cheek.

Shays speaks
I've really missed the whole gang ciss.
Cissy (still holding Shays)

I heard after the announcement Miller as the new Vice-President, you went bananas!! Personally I feel it, was a damn shame what Mr. Burlingame did!!

Shays
Yea Cissy! It really sucked.
Cissy (more angry)

You gave so much to this company to get treated like you did! Miller doesn't know from beans how to run this company!

Telephone rings

Cissy give Shays one last hug turns her head to Shays and gives him a friendly wave of "good bye" seats herself and continues her conservation on the telephone as Shays leaves her reception counter.

To Accounting Office

He walks down another corridor, which reveals personnel in each of them. He waves to a couple of them and continues down still another corridor until he reaches the accountant office.

Inside Accounting Office

He enters the office, which is well designed with expensive furniture, machines and computers. There is no one in the office as he takes a very close appraising view of his surroundings. He sees one of the computers shifting various information on the screen. He goes over to this screen and begins to read the daily report.

Shays speaks

Not doing too well in my absence are you Burlingame he sees the profits and margins of Auturo Engineerings' status. He sees salaries of all the employees including the President, owners Burlingame and Vice President Craig Miller. A one with all of these names, are names of employers who are making very low salaries.

Shay (again seating himself)

Got some fine people who are making some very, very poor salaries, Let's see if we can make some bank account changes. Let's call it…. profit sharing. That's good ha. Ha. He shifts sums of money from Auturo Engineering to Bank Accounts to at least 25 of the lower paid employees in the name of profit--sharing. A series of bank account numbers are passed directly to various banks-the banks respond by computer information is accepted and verified. Shays accepts all the income data on the print out machine as the noise begins to slow down. He rises from his seat, hits a last couple of licks on the computer returning it to its original pattern.

Let's see if you can live with this Burlingame!!!

He eases out of the accounting office and into the corridor. As he turns to go into the second winding corridor he passes, he sees an unfamiliar face. She is relatively attractive and in her late 30's. She is also caring business files and a cup of coffee. Shays turns and speaks.

Shays
Who might you be? Charlene speaks
I'm Charlene, who are you?

Shays
And what do you do Charlene?

Charlene
I'm the accountant.

Shays
I suppose you'll be leaving soon for the holiday?

Charlene (looking at her watch)
Yep! In about ten minutes for 2 weeks…you need something?

Shays
No Charlene, but I do hope you enjoy your holidays…

Shays turns and continues his leaving as Charlene gives a curious look at him; she turns takes a sip of her coffee and goes to her office.

European Resort

Another dynamic musical interlude which brings one to the opposite end of the globe in Europe. Levi Burlingame and his wife Trevor are enjoying the best that France has to offer as they drink large glasses of spirits.

They recline in their recliners-dressed in swim-wear near a beautifully shaped pool.

Mr. Burlingame

Ahhhhh! Trevor my dear! We must do this more often. This is the real life!

Trevor speaks for the first time: Trevor

Yes Levi this is truly a remarkable atmosphere. (sipping from her glass)

Burlingame (continues)

You know, with the kind of money I make, I should be able to do this sort of thang 2 or 3 times a year!

Trevor

Yes Levi this is truly a remarkable atmosphere. Levi...
There's been something bothering me...

Burlingame

I know...I know. My decision to make my dear friend and trusted associate, Miller, my Vice-President of Auturo-Engineering, instead of Shays Barker.

Trevor

Shays has given you his loyalty and skills for 10 long years. You've put him on some of our worst contracts and...he always came through for us.
(sitting up looking directly at Levi)
There is an interruption by a Bus Boy who gives both of them a fresh glass and clears away the excess. The Bus Boy gestures courtesy as he leaves the Burlingame's presence.

Trevor

You could call him anytime day..or Night! He was always there for us!! You said you were going to make him Vice President...What made you change your mind???

Mr. Burlingame

Trevor – we're thousands of miles away from the states. Here we are in one of the most beautiful places in the entire world…so let's enjoy t it!!!

Trevor (coming right back)

And with what we made from Shays work…He should be able to go anywhere in the world!

Burlingame (now very angry)

Look!!! There was a decision to be made…and I made it! So I changed my mind so what??

Trevor (at the height of her anger)

Oh yes! I know what you mean Levi. He's a mirror of everything you are not. He could work his tail to the bone for us…but gets no promotion! (She grabs her towel, lotion and sunglasses)

Burlingame (reacting)

I think you're taking this whole thing much too seriously

Trevor

Too seriously? - (Throwing her glass to the ground)
Burlingame stands suddenly as he looks at the shattered glass on the ground.
Burlingame

For Christ's sake Trevor!!

I don't get the feeling your friend Miller possess the skills or aggressiveness Shays has. You see…he still has to learn about how our company works…and that's gonna take a whole lot of time.

Trevor turns from her husband and heads toward the outside steps part of the way up she turns and speaks again.

Trevor

Right never wronged anybody Levi…this decision you made…I have every reason to believe you're going to live to regret it…. seriously regret it!!

Trevor turns and heads toward the upper level of the resort as Burlingame turns and goes back to his recliner. He put his dark sunglasses back on-lies back and relaxes.

Heavy soul beats of music interlude. Days pass-period, intervals as Mrs. Burlingame is in the pool, lots of music plays at this junction.

Levi and Trevor Burlingame's Return from England

As Levi and Trevor return through their security area and is admitted through security they observe the beautiful homes. Levi drives the Rose Royce through winding streets. The crooks and turns takes them higher and higher until if they wind up finally on their street. Levi is first to speak as he comes up where he normally stops.

(Levi-looking back and forth)

Where's <u>our</u> house? Where's <u>my</u> house??!!

Trevor gets out of the car leaving the door open and screams Levi----Levi------ where's our beautiful-Where is it?? Oooh No!! No!! There is nothing to be seen but acres of green land. No one could tell a <u>$15,000,000</u> <u>Mansion</u> once occupied much of this now green space.

Trevor screams-screams a <u>shrill cry</u> as she is totally devastated. She runs on her land and turns as though the mansion is going to reappear right in front of her eyes. It does not. She sinks to the grass and gives more of her shrill cries...

COURT ROOM SETTING

The courtroom is jammed packed with curious expectations. The principals Mr. & Mrs. Burlingame, their 2 attorneys Bromley & Stiles, Shays Barker, his 2 black female lawyers…. Monica Green & Glenda Reese, the Court Reporter & Clerk several Deputies and a host of Newspaper Reporters who are coming up to the principal and taking pictures with their flash cameras are present.

As the judge enters, the clerk asks all present to rise.

CLERK BANES

Will everyone please rise?!! (The crowd rises) (The judge enters to the chair). The honorable Judge Queen King is now presiding

The crowd remains standing as the Judge takes her position. She stands and looks over in her crowded courtroom. She is a Black-Woman in her mid-40's. She is about 4' ft & 10' in height as she stands sternly at her huge crowd, she speaks.

JUDGE-QUEEN KING

My name is Judge Queen King. (from the crowd there is laughter. She continues) There has been presented to my courtship one of the most extraordinary and daring violations of moral dignity and legal content known to man. I have been a Judge for 21 years and never, never has a case of this nature graced my courtroom. My interest is to arrive at a guilty or innocent verdict.

I don't care if you are Black or White. Justice will be served here in my courtroom, and I am on the side of Justice! Everyone here will be quiet and disciplined. This is most unusual case, and we are going to need your cooperation to get through it. I have been called a no nonsense Queen…maybe before this is all over with…. you too will know why. Judge Queen hits down on her gavel 2 times. You may take your seats. Her audience takes their seats as flashes of light re-occur.

Judge Queen (angrily)

My first order!! To all photographers – No pictures in my courtroom!!!….(all flashes stop)

Now there has been tremendous notoriety surrounding this case. The newspapers..television..This case could be easily dubbed…The case of the Missing Mansion.

(Some in agreement from the audience..but Judge Queen hits down on her gavel immediately 3 times) All right let's get on with this. Mr. Prosecuting Attorney your opening statements please!

COURTROOM SETTING

Prosecuting Attorney Bromley stands, as Attorney Monica Green and Mr. & Mrs. Burlingame remain seated at their tables.

(Prosecuting attorney Bromley)

Judge Queen. I, like you, have never had a case of this extraordinary nature. It just be-fuddles the human mind to present a case like this to court.

Judge Queen

Yes, Yes Mr. Prosecutor....But you will won't you. Present your case I mean?

Attorney Bromley (quickly recovering)

Of course! Of course your honor. I shall, Mr. and Mrs. Burlingame came home from their 3 month vacation in England 3 weeks ago only to discover...to discover (pausing)

Judge Queen

Yes only to discover...Go on counselor!

Attorney Bromley (nervously)

Only to...To discover their house –no their 13 room beautiful mansion had disappeared! (Long laughter from the audience)

Judge Queen (tapping on her gavel)

There is to be order or I will clear this courtroom.

Mr. Bromley

In addition to that, all of their household furnishing a tremendous wardrobe…. fabulous clothing for both of them 4 paintings by Masters & Jewelry.

At this remark Mrs. Burlingame begins to sob. There is an interruption again. Judge Queen looks at Mrs. Burlingame as the counselor starts again.

Mr. Bromley

I just for the life of me cannot understand how a house could disappear…a baby grand was even in the house (louder) this was a highly secured and a most exclusive area….Your Honor how could such a thing happen??

Judge Queen

That's why we are here in a court of Law isn't it counselor??

Mr. Bromley

There's more your Honor, All of Mr. & Mrs. Burlingame's credit cards with the banks & their company Auturo Engineering Assets were strangely depleted leaving the Burlingames in a state of Bankruptcy!!!

The charges from the Burlingames are, that one Shays Barker is responsible for these atrocities and he should be punished to the fullest extent of the law.

(Reading) The total extents of damages are in excess of 18____million dollars.

Remaining, as the Burlingames major assets are a $600.00 diamond ring watch Mr. Burlingame wears on his left hand. Mrs. Burlingames wears a necklace and a diamond ring valued at 1600.00. dollars

There is finally a late model Rose Royce at $91, 000 which they will have to literally pawn to pay attorney fees, unless Mr. Shays is found guilty they will not have moderate living expenses.

Flash – outside courthouse: Spectators check out Burlingame's Rose Royce (Then return to courtroom)

Judge Queen

Counselor your presentation has been so noted and as proper legal procedure dictates the court will now hear from the Defense – Flash- outside courthouse:

The Hispanic Father finally after checking sees Burlingame's Rose Royce goes over to the car, Looks around to see who is looking, he begins to pry_____the locks with his locks with his instrument. After a little difficulty the latch unlocks and he enters the car. He leans under the dash, pulls wires then attaches them the car starts up and he checks his surroundings then takes off. He drives to the nearest corner where his younger son awaits him. The car stops and his son gets in. The Rose speeds off into the distance. The Burlingame's <u>now</u> <u>don't</u> <u>even</u> <u>have</u> their $91, 000 Rose Royce.

Detectives Office

Lt. Rick Starlin of the Detective Bureau makes it clear in no uncertain terms to his two partners Deidra Paine and Wallace Fontaine. I shore, as hell can't figure it, and I've been on the force more than twenty years Fontaine.

A FIFTEEN MILLION DOLLAR MANSION just doesn't disappear into thin air!! And <u>NOBODY</u> sees it move at all. It just doesn't happen in the twentieth century.

<u>Fontaine speaks</u>

We've been out to the Burlingame's home-site several times...and not a trace of <u>foul play.</u>

Deidra who is trying to talk and open her stuck-desk drawer becomes frustrated. Starlin Fontaine! We are a tremendous team. When have we been unable to crack a case? (She stands at her desk shaking the draw which refuses to open). All that beautiful furniture-all those furs and jewelry gone.

Rick interjects with more certainty-don't forget their beautiful and very expensive Rose Royce...!!!

Deidra pauses and tries once again to open her lower right drawer. She bends showing her curvaceous hip-line. Detective Fontaine sees her situation and rises from his nearby desk-steps to Deidra's desk and tends to assistance her. He gently moves her aside, bends and bangs 2 times against the drawer. He then pulls the drawer open.

Deidra attempts to make another point of observation.

You know what really grabs me? If this had happened to <u>me</u>, I <u>still</u> wouldn't be able to go to the bank and get my money because some slick S.O.B. has depleted all my accounts!

Rick(interjects)

And you wouldn't have one single suspect: No evidence of any sort….No clues. It's as though <u>no crime has ever</u> been committed!!

Can you imagine the anger….the helplessness….Just the bitter… Bitter frustration of not being able to do anything….about anything??

<u>Diedra speaks</u>

Well we have never given up on a case. No matter how hard it was. And we sure as hell aren't giving up on this one. (She rises from her desk reaches for her coat). Let's go guys----

PARK SCENE

On a very pleasant day at a park a little black girl around 3 years old is seen climbing an obstacle play unit a short distance away, is a Caucasian boy that looks to be around 7 years old bouncing his ball on the ground.

Some one standing behind bushes with a birds-eye view observes all of this. The observer also sees across from the 2 children playing, a woman seemingly in her forties. She is simply dressed which also reveals her well-shaped legs and an appealing figure. She wipes tears from her eyes as she sobs aloud.

The woman is Mrs. Burlingame . Moments pass as the observer watches those in the park. The little girl who is swinging on the top bar of the obstacle swings by her arms extended she now hangs from the over hang bar. She holds for a moment then releases her hands and falls to the ground. The observer moves from his position behind the bushes and approaches the little girl. He reaches her hand and kneels. He asks her if he can help. She replies. I'm alright.

Shays helps her up as she brushes herself off, what's your name, she asks?

Mr. Friend. That's a funny name, Mr. Friend, What's your name little girl? Trissy, would you like to be a friend to me, Trissy. Sure!! What would I have to do? See that little boy over there. Yep! Shays reaches in his pocket. He takes out a wrapped ring size box. Gives this to that little boy and tell him to give it to that lady sitting on the bench. O.K. Shays hands the box to Trissy. Are we friends now Mr. Friend? Yes-yes we are friends, now go-give it to him.

Trissy goes toward the boy as she turns Shays waves good by. Trissy waves good-by too.

Trissy gets closer to the boy but is startled by a dog that comes directly at her. She freezes but releases the ring- like box from her hand. As the dog gets closer to her she closes her eyes. Seconds pass and Trissy squints one eye open, there is no dog. The dog has passed her. She turns quickly and watches the dog run... She turns back and starts running toward the boy but stops abruptly and looks up at the sun… then runs back to where she closed her eyes, and starts looking for the box. Trissy's search is complete. She snatches it from the ground and runs down once again to the boy.

The boy continues dribbling the ball Hey Boy! Here! Hey Boy!… she extends her hand with the little box… in it. He doesn't stop bouncing the ball.

Park Scene 2

Trissy stands watching the boy bounce his basketball. After watching for a short spell Trissy decides to join into the boy's fun by reaching in and grabbing his ball. The boy stops abruptly screaming at Trissy. Give me my ball. Give me… my ball!!! Trissy turns from him and runs. The boy gives chase… and catches her as he snatches his ball from her screaming once again stop, melding!! As he turns from her, Trissy extends her hand holding the little box. Give this to that lady! What is it? (Pointing) That man over there said for you to give it to that lady. The boy accepts the box suspiciously-he looks around- I don't see no man! Trissy tells him again to go and give the box to the lady sitting on the bench. The boy looks around again and spies the woman. He takes another look at the box and begins to dribble his ball over to where she is seated- Trissy runs to her mother some distance away who is lying on the grass reading a book.

Park Scene 3

The boy approaches the bench where the lady is seated. Her eyes are in a saddened state. He starts dribbling the basketball. She reacts to his persistent bouncing of his basketball. Stop with that inferno noise!! He stops and stares at her. He looks at her and she looks at him. (?) Well what do you want?? He doesn't reply. (Angrily) Well what do you want??

Becoming somewhat alarmed at her scorn, the boy hands her the little box. After giving her the box he backs up slowly. What is this??

From a distance a woman's voice calls for Victor. Victor! The boy then turns and runs up hill to his mother who awaits him at their car.

Mrs. Burlingame unties the box then unwraps it. She slowly opens the box only to find her beautiful set of very expensive sapphire rings returned. She is so astonished she rises from her bench, her head falls back as she clutches the rings to her breast. As if to give thanks for their return.

Tears began to flow once again. Mrs. Burlingame rejoices in her moment of acceptance. She eventually____comes to herself and attempts to follow Victor. In her attempt to follow, she suddenly knocks the heel of her shoe off. She is truly rushing and yelling "Little boy – Little Boy!! But Victor has settled himself in his mother's car as she drives from the park.____ She takes the broken shoe off. She turns and rushes with only one shoe on and the broken shoe in one hand. She makes way to a little transportation car she has parked by the park. Moments pass as she awkwardly makes it to her car. She pauses at her car and takes another look at her rings,____ Throws her broken shoe in the car, jumps in, starts her car and joins the traffic with one shoe on and one shoe off.

TRAFFIC SCENE

As <u>Mrs. Burlingame</u> speeds through traffic careening around trucks, buses, and cars, one can see it is one tremendous scene, as she almost has several accidents. She drives several miles with tires screeching as she shifts using one bare – foot as assistance.

She finally screeches into her appointed destination. She jumps out of her car without putting the car in the proper gear and she fails to turn the motor off. The car begins to roll backwards. She has to turn <u>and</u> <u>run</u>   with one shoe on and one shoe off several paces from the car. She now realizes that she has got to get back to the car in a hurry. She runs in a funny fashion back to the car, jumps in before it hits a beautiful late model car. She stops the car shifts forward and goes back to her original parking space. She secures the car properly this time and gets out. She begins her teeter-totter up & down walk. But once again she stops a few feet from the car. She turns and rushes back to the passenger side of her car. She reaches through the open window and opens the glove compartment. She pulls a tape recorder hand model. She turns it on and there is music that plays for a few seconds. She stops the music rewinds the tape, she now clicks it on record and leaves it on.

Trevor drops it in her front dress pocket. She leaves her car and teeter totters her way hurriedly to a classy apartment door.

IN SHAYS APARTMENT

<u>Trevor</u> Knocks feverishly in the hope that the door will open. She continues <u>Knocking</u> to no avail. Still facing the door, she presses on the door. The door comes ajar. She hollers out <u>Shays-Shays</u> several times but there is no answer. She pushes the door wide and steps into Shays apartment.

Once inside <u>Trevor</u> screams his name with more anticipation. Still silence permeates the apartment.

_____She_____eases from the front door to the living room, which is neatly arranged with a sofa, chair, coffee table and assortment of inexpensive pictures on the wall. She checks the kitchen, which is in disarray with dirty pots & pans. There are dishes in the sink. She moves and checks the bathroom, which is also empty.

_____She_____moves further to the rear of the apartment to the bedroom. It is a relatively large bedroom and sprawled on top of a king size bed is the figure of a man dressed in nothing but briefs. He is lying on his stomach and his face is turned side ways. He appears sleep on his arm. She enters the room and goes directly to his bed._____Trevor_____ - stands over him as she views his well-developed masculine frame.

APARTMENT SCENE 2

As she looks at him slowly eases on the bed beside him. She now eyes his face attentively as he obviously is in deep sleep. She begins to run her hand through his curly hair. She strokes his shoulders and back ever so gently.

Moments pass as gently stroking continues._____Shays_____- begins to stir as she stops with her stroking and he_____now turns on his back, but continues to sleep. She cuddles closer to him as she once again looks into his face. Placing her hand around his cheek, she lowers her face to his and gives him a short kiss on his lips. She kisses him again with more passion. He slowly begins to respond by putting his arms under her and with his eyes still closed he kissed her back.

This kiss is momentary because at an instant he pushes her back. What is it?? Oh God, I thought I was dreaming…! Trevor!!-what are you doing here? I thought I was dreaming! She hushes him by putting her finger on his lips. As she reaches in her pocket she speaks gratefully – you gave me back my beautiful sapphires didn't you? "She shows the rings" You gave them back to me! You knew how much I loved my rings," At these remarks Shays climbs from the bed. "No!

Trevor – No! you are wrong!! You have me all wrong! "(Pulling away from her.)____

IN SHAYS APARTMENT –3

You took our home!! Our beautiful furniture! We lost our Rose Royce (she slopes off the bed to confront him) you left me and my husband Bankrupt!! But, (calmly) you know_____I understand why you did it…coming closer to him I really understand. (Angrily) I told Levi – that he should not have taken advantage of you…but he just wouldn't listen! Shays ____--Interrupts-Trevor please go home. This is no good. Trevor blurts out – you shoulda been Vice President of Auturo-Engineering you! - our company! Not that pompous, arrogant Assonine, Miller! So you see, Shays I did care about what happened to you and I still do care (she puts her hands on his shoulder as she now stands in front of him). I can remember when you used to come into my home and look at me in a very special way like…you wanted me, like you, wanted to make love to me. She falls gently into his arms and once again gives him a passionate kiss._____

Shays lifts her up in his arms takes her to his bed as she still wears the left foot shoe. He places her on the bed. Shays aggressively and proceeds to unbutton her silk blouse.____Trevor____continues her charm conversation…. you want me, don't you____Shays____? "___Trevor____" Cooperates by hurriedly removing her blouse exposing her very healthy bust covered by a brassiere.

APARTMENT - SCENE 4

_____Shays_____Proceeds to initiate a kiss on <u>Trevor's</u> neck and begins to slowly rub his hands on her side. As_____she_____ eases back_____He_____lies atop of her. He feels a hard object pressing against his leg. He reaches down to her pocket at which time_____she_____ does the same but his hand is first. (Nervously she speaks) "I've got it. But_____he_____doesn't remove his hand. He pushes her hand away and reaches inside. She tries to stop him but he is too strong. He pulls away from her holding the tape recorder in his hand, which is still recording. He puts the tape on stop, rewinds the tape and plays this message: you took our home! Our beautiful furniture even our Rose Royce. You left my husband and me bankrupt but you know_____I understand why you did it.

_____Shays_____interrupts by throwing the tape against the wall. You lying wrench you understand me!! You understand me!!

<u>She</u> sits with her head knelt at her knees knowing her plan of_____ (crying Trevor)_____I just want my clothes that's all. It took years to get that wardrobe. I just want my clothes._____Angrily Shays picks her blouse off the floor and grabs her off the bed by her arm and forcefully pulls her in her teeter-totter fashion from his bedroom to his front door. She is screaming to him, I do understand why you did it. I really do understand you!! Ignoringly_____Shays opens his front door physically shoves her out the door. Go home Mrs. <u>Burlingame!</u> <u>Go home to your husband Levi!!!</u> He slams the door-he takes a few steps away but he turns and rushes back…opens the door and throws her blouse in her face, then once again he slams the door!!

APT – 5

<u>Trevor</u> snatches the blouse from her face and cries at her loudest as she pounds on the door and screams at_____Shays_____, I want my clothes!!!_____I want my clothes!!! Still sobbing having a bra, dress and one shoe on... she sinks to her knees, please give me back my clothes!! Please give me back my clothes!!!

Mrs. Burlingame's Returns Homes.

Much rain pours down, as lighting strikes overhead in the downpour. Moments pass as Trevor crashes through her apartment door soaking wet. Still holding one shoe in hand she slams the door only to turn and greet her husband…Mr. Burlingame…who stands with a drink in one hand and stares suspiciously at his wife. I'm not going to ask, where the hell you have been he says in anger. With straggly hair over her face, dress torn and standing with one shoe she looks at him sternly and retorts, then don't ask…!! Trevor takes the drink from …Burlingame… gulps it down and hands the glass back to her husband and proceeds to leave him. Burlingame walks to his alcohol tray puts some ice in his glass, grabs the whiskey bottle and goes to his nearby chair & seats himself. He begins to talk to himself. I built an empire in 15 years I built a company that…. competes with the best of them… And now its destroyed, my home…destroyed now even my marriage…my damn marriage has gone down the tubes. He pours the whiskey in the glass and starts gulping it down. He pours more and drinks more…

Singles Apartment

Trevor paces back and forth nervously in their less than stylish singles apartment. As she expresses her anger over their continuous loss.

There's nobody on the planet goin' through the sorry, sorry mess I'm in. Trevor reaches inside the old-type refrigerator for milk.

Oh God – where the hell is the milk? She holds a less than half full quart container. Almost at her last wits she throws the container into the sink.

She suddenly turns from the sink and blurts out you never!! Never should have let this happen!! But you did…didn't you? We lost our beautiful – beautiful home… I lost all my expensive jewelry mister!! Oh my God, my fabulous wardrobe…All gone!

Tears stream from Trevor's eyes – damn our bank accounts are in mere shambles.

She points her finger (nervously) at Mr. Burlingame who is seated at the small table in their very small kitchen. Sipping on coffee.

We're living in this cesspool hole of nothingness because we can't do any better. We're the Burlingame's remember? The family who went from Riches to Rags!!! Hell! We don't even have transportation to our grocery store because some slick S.O.B. stole our (she pauses) well it was just our Rose Royce. Mr. Burlingame sits silently as he runs his hands through his hair – then bows and shakes his head in total rejection.

Mr. Burlingame takes a deep breath and begins to sip again on his coffee. Trevor at this point although factual is determined to be equally obnoxious once again. She screams at Burlingame-We have lost everything!! We have nothing!! Levi do something! Don't just sit there sippin on that damn coffee somebody stole our life!!! Angrily she slaps the hot coffee out of his hand. Mr. Burlingame jumps up trying to keep from scalding himself. He shakes his hand quickly. Trevor. Trevor get a hold of yourself! Mr. Burlingame speaks for the first time but his appeal for Trevor to calm down is in vain because she grabs his jacket that was hanging over the chair next to the one in which he was sitting. Mr. Burlingame caught by surprise tried to speak again-Trevor have you gone… Trevor interrupts as she open the door. Levi somebody stole our money, go out and find out who. Go find our money!! She physically pushed her husband out the door. He offers little resistance. She slams the door as Mr. Burlingame stands coat in hand with a perplexed expression on his face.

Barly Mason Equity Business & Loans

Mr. Burlingame enters the exclusive company <u>Barly Mason Equity & Business Loan.</u> Once inside he can see that this company is truly successful by its décor and well dressed personnel. As he passes various offices he stops himself at the calling out of his name.

Barly Mason
Hey Levi!

Mr. Burlingame having passed Mr. Mason's office turns and comes back to the well statued well attired with diamond rings, gold watch-president of Barly Mason Equity & Business Loans.

<u>Barly Mason</u>

Its so good to see ya Levi (extending his hand) How long has it been?? Burlingame shakes Mr. Mason's hand as Mr. Mason heads him into his lavishly furnished office.

Burlingame (seating himself)

Been about 5 years Barly. How is that pretty
wife of yours? Pretty as she used to be?

Burlingame

She's still the same just highly upset lately.

<u>Mason</u>

Looking around Mason's office Burlingame is truly impressed you've come along way since I last saw you Barly.

<u>Mason</u>

You remember Levi... when I came to you with a brand new concept in a plumbing system?? I literally begged you to just take a look you wouldn't even consider it for one minute.

Burlingame

I remember you were really pressing with that idea you called it your Revolutionary plumbing system. I'm sorry Barly.

Barly

Don't matter now. Those were my hungry days. Believe me it took years after you turned me down to find the right hook up.

Burlingame

How did you finally make your contract?

Barly

Strangest thang Levi-2 Australian guys came into a bar I was in. I overheard one of them say that his holdings in America were up for some serious taxation from the I.R.S... unless he could pay off some of his principal earnings.

Barly goes back to his computer. He starts once again typing on it as if to see if he can register up more information. The conversation has ceased between them but Levi is obviously more nervous than ever because now as he sits right before Barly, he pats his left foot continuously in a steady rhythmic pattern with both his hands tapping each other in that same pattern or timing as his foot.

<u>Barly (stops to speak)</u>

A man's house and banks accounts just disappear and nobody knows what happened!! Man that is awesome. At this point Mr. Burlingame appears angry stands and leans toward Barly at his desk. You're not going to make me wait and put me through what you put your other applicants through. Are you? Levi-business is business! I had to go through this routine year after year nobody said, just because my name is Barly Mason-oh you don't you don't have to go through this or that:

<u>(Levi returns)</u>

I'm just asking for a $350,000 loan. My home, my business for the past 20 years should count for something.

<u>(Barly returns)</u>

You don't have a <u>home</u> or <u>business</u> accounts anymore!!

To me he was a God sent. I immediately introduced myself and told then that they could use my entire plumbing system from a corporate stand point. Finance the entire business corporation of Barly Mason Equity and business loans. They would get the taxation relief they need and I would finally get my new system up and running in the main stream and have it running. Levi. What has been happening to you Levi? I've been hearing all sorts of things about your business. And what's this I hear about your fantastic mansion disappearing.

Burlingame

I've tried to explain it to myself and it just doesn't come out right. The ground my home was on has nothing but acres of grass. As though my home was never there!!

Mason

Wow!! It sounds like something out of fantasy. Well its not a fantasy!! This is the 21st century-this is real life! My wife and I were wealthy people-I had a real life home a thriving business my bank accounts were huge (wiping his eyes with his hand (chief)...

That's why I'm here Barly I need help in the worst way....I need your help Barly.....

Barly looks at Mr. Burlingame not with compassion but more curiosity. Moments pass as Barly checks the computer that sits adjacent his desk. He writes some information on his scratch pad tears a sheet off and summons his executive secretary to his office. Mr. Burlingame sits in silence although observing with great anticipation. After speaking through the telephone system Barly's secretary enters. She is a rather stately woman all attractive woman with long back hair.

Rosine

Yes Mr. Mason. You need what at the moment? Barly hands Rosine the sheet of paper he wrote on.

<u>Barly</u>

Check this out through all <u>our automated systems</u> right away Rosine.

Rosine (as she turns to leave) I'll get right on it Mr. Mason.

Rosine enters once again with several sheets consisting of computer read outs. She hands the paper to Barly as he scans what is written. He begins to read from the paper. Credit Analysis indicate that Mr. Levi Burlingame present accounts with 6 institutions-0000 and 0 one 2002 fully equipped Rose Royce stolen. Property at 921 Stouter Dr. Banner heights valued at 15 million: disappeared. Cannot appraise considers Levi Burlingame's present status too risky to loan: disapproved.

Mr. Burlingame (stands up)

Oh for Christ sake Barly!! You're not going to let me walk out of here the same way I walked in with-nothing?

Barly (approaches Levi)

Hell no Levi! We can't let you have the big money- (Barly reaches in his pocket and pulls out enough money to choke the average horse. He pulls from the pack a $50.00 bill). Take this; he places the money in Levi's lapel pockets). I'm sorry you've had the worst kind of luck. He leads Burlingame back to his front door. You have to admit one thing Levi; I did more for you than you ever did for me. Burlingame stunned stands and looks at Barly, then at Rosine, then hastily passes Barly.

Burlingame's Walk to 3 Sisters Home

Mr. Burlingame walks down an urban sidewalk tiredly. With his coat slung over his shoulder he stops at a well deserved??? Leans one arm on it and wipes his handkerchief over his face. He takes a deep breath and proceeds to his destination, which is at the door of 3 sisters. He presses a chime bell. The bell chimes to a melodious beat. There is no response. Burlingame becomes more impatient knocks and rings the bell chimes once again. The eye-latch on the door opens just enough for him to see an eye from the inside looking directly at him.

The door opens and a woman who appears to be in her sixty's speaks. Well, after 12 years look what the cat drug up to our doorsteps!

Hello Gladys-it's been a long time. Gladys is dressed in a long green gown. Her short silver looking hair appears to have just recently been done. She's rather tall and slender in statue. Somewhat agitated she opens the door even wider.

Come on in Levi. I haven't seen you in a coons-age. Leona. Maxine! Just look whose here!

Maxine comes to the dining room followed by Leona. Maxine, about 50 and heavier set than Gladys. She is shorter and wears a dark pants suit. Leona looks the youngest about the same height as Maxine. Oh you remember my 2 sisters Leona and Maxine? She's just a little heavier than Gladys. Maxine yells-If it's not the running GIGOLO!! And where's Trevor??

<u>Burlingame</u>

She's <u>not</u> with me. I'm just glad to see all of you.

(<u>Leona speaks</u>)

What do you mean she's not with you??

(<u>Maxine</u>-blurts out)

You mean Ms. Goody two shoes left you? Like you left my sister <u>Gladys</u>, years back?? Burlingame has not been asked to sit down. All four of them stand as Maxine takes personal jabs at him.

You look a little worn and beat-up…(more sternly) Why are you here Levi?? Gladys I need help…. I'm sorry about how things turned out…. back then.

Gladys'

You mean back when I was your fiancée. Back when we were to be <u>married</u> just a few days before <u>Miss Pretty</u> <u>face</u> Trevor started her campaign to get you…and she finally got you too!!

(<u>Burlingame tries to speak</u>)

Gladys that was a long time ago.

<u>Gladys Retorts</u>

Not for me. I counted everyday. Thinking you may come back. It hasn't been that long. There hasn't been a day I haven't felt the pain… that nagging heartache that comes when you care for some-one you love so deep…and it hurts real deep!!

<u>Burlingame</u>

I didn't come to open up old wounds.

<u>Gladys</u>

You dropped me faster than I can spit Levi?

<u>Now Leona speaks up (Merely)</u> Didn't you love my sister??

Maxine-Interrupts with sure he did Leona...that's why he left her!!

Burlingame

Ooh for Christ sakes. Look...Look...(nervously) I need your help Gladys. I <u>need</u> a loan!! I <u>will</u> pay you back!!

Pay me back-Pay me back?? <u>Levi</u>- (Growing more desperate)

Every since I've known you Gladys you have a lot of money. I just want you to help me out of this jam with a loan---------

<u>Leona</u>

We must have done twenty miles of walkin' and shoppin'— shoppin' and walkin'!!

<u>Gladys</u>

Lord sending out all those invitations and tryin to find the right minister. The right church. You made a fool out of me Levi.

<u>Now </u>here you are plain as day. Haven't heard from you in ages... Battered and torn.... and in need of <u>my</u> money!!

Leona-Inquires

Gladys. Are you going to give Levi some money?? Gladys has become a little teary eyed and begins to wipe her eyes with her handkerchief. She turns from the three of them and as she wipes streaming tears from her face, he makes this declaration.

No!! I'm not giving up one red-cent!! Leona at this instance moves to open the front door as Levi Burlingame tries to make a <u>last appeal</u> for the money.

<u>Levi</u>

Try to find it in your heart Gladys. Help me-I need it bad!!!

<u>Gladys</u>- (teary eyed & shaken voice)

No! I won't do it. Good-bye Levi!!
Levi once again is stunned and pauses in silence. As Leona opens the door <u>wide</u> for his departure. He turns and slowly makes his way through the door. Leona slams the door behind him. Bam!!!
Maxine simply says. What a shame!!! And you <u>still love him</u>!!
Leona and Maxine look upon Gladys tearful but <u>expressionless</u> face.

Exhaustion sets in for Levi Burlingame

Burlingame walks down various streets-overpasses and railroads underpasses as <u>night</u> rain catches him.

<u>Thundershowers</u> of the heaviest kind come down and catches him mid-way a second railroad over-pass. As he stumbles through slush and nearly knee-deep water. Levi grows weary and weakens to his knees. While on knees he remembers the $50.00 bill Mr. Mason placed in his left shirt pocket. He pulls out the water soaked <u>unusable</u> bill that begins to wash away. The last of the bill washes away. He screams Lord God!! Why me??

Why me?? He crumbles to the sitting position in a whimpering state.

The thunderstorm strikes with lightning flashing as Levi Burlingame sits in a large puddle of water by a train yard track in an underpass. He tilts his head back on the underpass wall as the rain blows in and smacks his face....

At 6:15 A.M.

A squad car pulls up to Trevor's door. The officer leaves his car and proceeds to ring the bell. Trevor is sound asleep but the ringing and banging eventually arouses her. She climbs out of the bed rather reluctantly. She pulls her robe off the bed and puts it on.

In a very sleepy fashion she yawns and makes her way to the door. She stumbles to the door as the ringing and banging at the door continues. She yells through the door-Stop that <u>damn</u> noise!! Trevor peeps through her peephole. What are you doing at my door?? Officer Marly Ma'am. Are you Mrs. Trevor Burlingame? Yes. (with high anticipation) Would you open the door please? She opens the door and officer Marly speaks. Two railroad engineers found your husband Levi Burlingame.... well he was lying by the railroad tracks in an underpass in a pool of water. He's at City General Hospital. He has double pneumonia. Doctors say this is from exposure. You know we had one of the worst storms of the year last night. Trevor shows no particular reaction to the depressing news of her husband.

If you like, I can run you to the hospital.

<u>Trevor speaks</u>

Thank you, but don't bother. I'll get there.

<u>Officer Marly</u>

I certainly hope everything turns out ok. Goodbye.

He turns and leaves. Trevor closes the door. She walks slowly to her bed. She removes her robe and climbs <u>back</u> into bed…and pulls the <u>cover over</u> her head.

Shays Barker Remorse

Shays Barker enters his apartment from the street. The weather has been wet and drizzly. When he comes inside he leans back on the door and one can see his wet hair, face and clothes. He has on his face grimace and remorse almost to tears. He seems to have taken on another persona, which is a far cry from Shays Barker, the construction engineer who adopts the attitude of high aggression and confidence. The technician who with the <u>precision</u> of a <u>surgeon</u> who skillfully and meticulously slices up brains, hearts, lungs and kidneys...has nothing on him. Shays does the same on houses.

He ambles his way to his kitchen where he leans against his refrigerator. When a bad person does something bad against a <u>good</u> person. The bad person usually doesn't feel any real guilt. But when a good person (even in retaliation) then... a lot of guilt and remorse comes into play. You can't do <u>evil</u> for <u>evil</u> without there being serious repercussions. As with Shays Barker, he now begins to feel the brunt of his guilt.

Remors 2

Shays has been a good man all his life-at the Beck and call mostly-from the owners of the engineering establishment where he worked diligently over 17 years.

Shays now finds himself at odds with the very people he had grown to respect over the years.

If only Levi and Trevor Burlingame had seen fit to treat him fairly. Shays was not only a good man but an <u>exceptional</u> man and an <u>extraordinary</u> engineer...once and always at their beck and call. But the mounting pass-overs down through the years made something snap...snaps to the point of nothing but total revenge. He was left with only one desire...<u>To totally demoralize the Burlingame's</u>. To completely take everything they own and leave them with nothing... nothing at all!

Remors 3

Shays pulls away from the refrigerator-stands straight up and looks with a dead-man expression. He simply stands and stares... Moments pass as he slowly slithers to his knees, bows his head and clasps his fists under his chin in a prayer-like manner. He begins a mournful prayer.

Now I lay me down to sleep..I pray the Lord...I pray the Lord my soul to take (tears begin to appear) Lord I'm so sorry for what I have done. I'm sorry—I'm so terribly sorry.

(Louder) I don't know what happened! I just got so mad-madder than hell-oh excuse me Lord. (Shays at this moment has knelt even closer to the kitchen floor) Please forgive me.... forgive me I'm not a bad person. I'm not I'm not!!

Hospital room of Burlingame and Jayson—

Levi lies in a hospital room with his head back on a pillow. Sweat streams from his face as his eyes remain closed at the tapping and rhythmic noise from the African young man who seems to be around 19 years old. It's obvious that he has had a serious leg injury because his left leg is in a cast and raised. Noise intensifies as Jayson traps in his favorite beat with his ink pen against his dinner plate. He spurts our rap-phrase---after rap phrases. One can see he really gets into his groove...Louder and louder.

Nurse Priscilla rushes into the room. Jayson ----Jayson if you don't stop that noise!! She goes immediately over to Levi. He appears to still be sleep. She checks his vital signs and adjusts his medical apparatus. She moves to the young teenager and puts her finger to her mouth in-a quiet manner. She lifts his food tray and leaves the room.

Jayson who has been quiet all during Nurse Priscilla's presence. He gives the look of a young man who has just been scolded by a parent. Now he glances over to Levi's bed. Aha!! You finally opened your eyes! I guess it was my singin-huh? How long I been here?? God I feel so tired. Well you been here 3 days—Three days?? What happened to me? Hold it with the questions man. I came here about a day before you. Heard a couple of the nurses talkin. Said the police found you down near some railroad track....passed out....in a pool of water. Levi completely surprised and embarrassed turns completely away from his young informant. God! How stupid of me-I couldn't think of anything better to do!! Anybody been here to see me? Other than the hospital people... Nobody.

"With that storm and all the other nights, I'd say you were blessed being found in all that water. You know you caught double pneumonia."

Nurse Priscilla enters with Dr. Duran following.

Well it looks like our patients eyes have finally opened. And it appears Doctor-he's been engaging in conversation with our young noisy patient. The nurse and the doctor proceed to the bed of Levi Burlingame. They begin to check him leaving young Jayson once again alone in silence....Just looking.........

Jayson and Levi Burlingame Centered in the Hospital Cafeteria

Our young 19-year-old African-American Jayson is seated in his wheelchair with his broken leg extended over the foot-rest. He and Levi Burlingame are seated in the hospital cafeteria as they munch on sandwiches and sip on sodas. Ten days have passed since Levi entered the hospital and their association has grown somewhat close. It is obvious that Levi has expressed to Jayson some of the personal and tragic events that have occurred in his life.

So you see Jayson, (Levi sips on his soda) everything that has happened to me these past few weeks have been a shocker for me and beyond my....beyond my control!

Jayson responds

...And in spite of all those millions you made you can't get any money from nobody...you can't borrow no money from nobody to help you get on your feet??

Levi

I'm as much surprised as you Jayson!

Jayson

But with all those millions and millions you made...didn't you help sanybody???

Levi

I didn't give it much thought when I had the huge contracts..and making big money hand over fists...I have to face facts now!

Levi and Jayson In the Hospital Cafeteria

Jayson (interrupts)

So that's why they found you laid-out in a puddle of water by some railroad tracks...you went way up the ladder.... way up.... then you came down fast with a crash!!

Levi

I'd say that's the jist of it....In a nutshell.

Jayson (comes back to an

But why didn't you help somebody? One somebody?

Levi

Jayson....I've been through hell....This has been a big lesson to me. If I had to do it all over again....I'd do it much better.

Jayson (still rubbing it in)

Well you've been here nine days and you haven't had any visitors-not even from your wife. You don't have any friends-no transportation-no real place to stay.

Levi and Jayson about to leave hospital cafeteria-

Jayson and Levi just sit in silence as they finished sipping and eating their sandwiches. Jayson watches Levi suspiciously as Levi just sits and watches Jayson.

I don't know whether I wanna be your friend or not Levi.

I remember I used to need jobs from people like you. You know like <u>down</u> on my luck. I used to have ideas on music projects and I'd take them to offices like you had….those executives in their swanky offices would take one look at me and tell their secretarys-tell that boy to come back some other time or tell him we're not interested. They wouldn't have the slightest idea of what I had to offer. Now those were some heart breaking times for me!!!

Shays at the waterfront

10 months later----

A tall figure of a man in a Catholic suit with a thick wide white collar is seen throwing peanuts over the rail in the water to the sea gull at the water front on a beautiful sunshiny day. After throwing the food in the water as the birds circle and dip the man turns around. It is obvious he is a Black man ....obviously of Catholic persuasion. Children running on the wharf while playing run into the priest. Of all the children running into the priest one of them stops and says, I'm sorry Father" He takes off running again as the priest raises his hand in blessing and says, "Blessed are the children" where would this world be without them?"

On The Waterfront 2

As the Priest_____turns from the rush of the children, he hears a call-Father – Father. He looks around as he walks down the boardwalk. Sea Gulls fly overhead as the brisk wind blows and the sun shines on this very beautiful day. The voice in the distance calls even louder, Father!! The priest catches where the voice comes from this time and stops. He sees standing high up on a bleacher like landing the figure of a man. The man waves his arm as the priest sees him and heap in his direction. The man steps down the bleachers as the Priest who has now reached the bleachers takes his first few steps up toward the approaching man. They finally meet as the man extends his hand he says I'm sorry, but I must talk to you! The Priest extends his hand. They shake, I'm Father De-Wayne. I'm sorry; I'm Shays Barker, Father. Shays appearance shagged and tacky. His face un-shaven and his hair is uncombed. "You appear to be in dire need of help my son" What is it? What matter is it that is of such extreme urgency?

(Blurting out)

I have nightmares. Just about every night too! Night after night, nightmares. (Shays get more excited as he explains loudly) I can't sleep!! Let's take a seat. Father De-Wayne seats himself on the bleachers. Shays seats himself right next to him. "Now start from the beginning <u>and tell me</u> Shays Barker I want to hear it all.

On The Waterfront 3

Shays jumps up from his seat; they shouldn't have done this to me…. Father they shouldn't have done it!!! Easy…Easy my son, start from the very beginning.

Shays very angrily but proceeds – I worked very hard from my company for 17 long years and they passed me up 3 times hear me 3 times!! I was always there for them day and night!

This last time they passed me up, they brought in this outsider!! He didn't know beans about the job! I should have done the job, Shays Barker. Father I swore vengeance on the whole damn company.

So you did what, Shays Barker? I worked out a plan to destroy the company and even my boss's home! And how would you go about such a task?? I knew one of the best ways to bankrupt any company is to send company money to employees through profit sharing. Just send thousands of dollars to large numbers of workers. Using a Company Computer the company would soon go under. I knew the right time to get to the computers and make the transfers through various banking institutions.

Our company had tremendous credit so there was approval. Even above our total assets. Bankruptcy would come and it did real soon.

On The Waterfront 3

I was like a man on a mission out to search and destroy. My boss's home was my next target (Shays pauses) you have to understand Father, I am a good-hearted man. I have never deliberately hurt anyone in my life. The Priest's reacts. (Until) Now! I have been filled with so much vengeance and so much anger and hatred!

I planned my way into his home. I knew he would be on vacation for 2 or 3 months. I put a new sewage line that he had wanted in for several months. It was a very messy and stagnating job but he wanted <u>me</u> to do it.

His home was worth around. I took everything out, wardrobe. Jewelry, paintings, all his furnishings and then I started dismantling his home. Piece by piece and brick by brick. It took just 12 days to go from an <u>exclusive mansion with an</u> – exquisite setting… to a <u>clear field.</u> Father can you imagine going home…. To no home!! No home at all!!!

So it was you who was responsible for that home disappearing. That was the one on television and in the newspapers? Such a fantastically beautiful setting – and now a family is without their home or security.

(Priest Rising) In all my years in the priesthood I have never heard such a diabolical confession.

There's more Father Dewayne.

His wife came to my home, to my bed. She offered me her body. Also I took her husband's $91,000 Rose Royce. Now his insurance has lapsed.

I hope I <u>never</u> have the feelings again as I have had these past few days.

Father DeWayne standing as he expresses himself to Shays.

"What you have said staggers the imagination Shays Barker, Surely as God is above, the works of the devil have prevailed upon your soul.

(Firmly) Do you want the truth my son? The real truth? Yes.. Yes Father I want you to give me…(Priest DeWayne interrupts) <u>Absolution</u>? No I will not give you absolution for you to go away feeling justified and content for premeditating & committing some of the worst atrocities known to man, and there is no doubt in my mind you had <u>just cause</u> for real anger having been passed up on your job for the third time. You had just cause to challenge or to dispute…I could even understand if a fight took place. But to bankrupt a company and totally- totally dismantle a man's home. To just rape him and his family of all earthly possessions….what manner of rage possessed you my son??? Reaching inside his robe he pulls put a bible and begins to quote passages. Blessed are the meek - for they shall inherit the earth – blessed are the peacemaker….

Jayson and Levi Out of The Hospital

Several days late-Jayson is seen riding atop a grass-cutter. As he cuts, one can see that it is quite a view of an estate. He decides to drive his grass-cutter close to the side of the estate building where he comes upon Levi. Levi is standing on a short ladder trimming the hedges. Jayson cuts the motor off and speaks to Levi.

Well! It hasn't been all bad...has it Levi? Levi stops his wacking and turns to face Jayson. I don't know whether that agreement we made was a good one. I'm hot! I'm thirsty-here I am baking in the sun. I never had to do this...I don't have to do this!

(Jayson reacts)

Ooh yes you do....we both do!!! Dr. Duran gave us a golden chance to make some money...get a nice place n' pay our doctor bills. I could be home with my mother and her 5 kids. (Levi speaks)

You told me you don't want to be there.

(Jayson)

You're right......Not with 3 girls and 2 bad ass boys. Besides my mother needs money too. We made an agreement and we shore as hell better stick to it! Now let's get back to work.

Jayson starts his machine up and darts off. Sweat pours off of Levi. He wipes his brow-turns and continues working.

Much grass cutting is done along wide areas. The trimming of hedges by Levi continues-Levi also is seen drinking soft drinks and returns to work. He takes a shovel and starts bagging excess grass. As days go by Levi and Jayson have bags of grass on their shoulders and are walking toward the dumpster. The weather is extremely hot as Jayson limps noticeably but works diligently. The two of them make quite a working team. Night-inside motel

It is dark and Jayson and Levi are in a run-down motel room. There are 2 beds-a refrigerator-a hot plate-a small 2 seat table. There are holes in the wall and a small bathroom. Levi is showering in the bathroom while Jayson is preparing dinner. Jayson has a towel wrapped around him like an apron-towel effect. He dabs a little pepper and salt into the pot he has simmering on the hot plate. Moments pass and the shower stops-Levi is drying himself off, as it is obvious he is not in the best of mood. He speaks <u>aloud</u> behind the bathroom door, which is partially open.

I tell you Jayson...every part of my body aches. This is the worst feelin I've had in my entire life.

Jayson responds

I know this is some kind of change for you Levi...you never had to, as they say in the streets. Bite the bullet.... But my mother and me...my whole family has had to bite the bullet every day----------

Jayson is now pouring from the pot into 2 bowls. Levi comes out of the bathroom with the towel wrapped around him. God I hurt everywhere!! And just look at me. I have dined at the most elaborate- the most luxurious places and with the exclusive of people.

Jayson interrupts

Yeah- And not one of those exclusive people would help you when you needed it most. Now listen I'm in pain- don't you think I'm hurtin too??

Let's cut out all of this jabberin and eat something. Levi is sitting on his bed with his towel wrapped around him drying his head with a hand-cloth. He inquires. What's for dinner?

Jayson walk over to Levi with a tray.

Ooh jeeze..Oohh jeeze-more soup, crackers, and bananas?

Jayson speaks

And ice cold water!!

So this what I'm breaking my back for. Jailbirds eat better than this!

Jayson-seated at the table-

Yeah and anyone of those jailbirds would like to <u>trade places </u>with you Levi. Don't worry we've got to squeeze this little change we made to the next check.

God! When will this nightmare end? What did I do to deserve this?? You didn't treat people right and it's called payback!!

Heyy! I just thought of something Levi. We have another job!!!

<u>Levi</u>

Jayson I don't want to hear-don't please don't.

<u>Jayson continues</u>

I was talking with the owner of this motel…a really nice guy and he said he was going to straighten up this motel and had a whole lot of painting that needs to be done.

<u>Levi</u> (sarcastically)

Soo-------

<u>Jayson</u>

So he said if we wanted to pay for our stay here-well if we would paint. He would give us our rent free-we wouldn't have to pay.

<u>Levi</u>

I'm no painter-besides I ache too much to try-----

<u>Jayson</u> –retorts

You listen to me Levi. We're getting a break. I volunteered us and you're goin to be one of the greatest painters of the century!!!!

Jayson and Levi are already committed to the maintenance of Dr. Duran's estate but have also agreed to work for Mr. Moreland who owns the Moreland Motel. Dr. Duran's work will be done during the weekdays and Mr. Moreland's work will be done a few hours in the evenings and weekends.

Both of them are seen rolling paint on the outside of the motel. Up & down the two of them go as paint is being smoothed out on the exterior wall.

Mr. Moreland a tall slender man approximately 60 years of age watches attentively as they work. Jayson is again enthusiastic about his latest business venture.

Just think of it Levi! We sparkle up Mr. Moreland's motel and we don't pay any rent. We do our regular gig with Dr. Duran then we come here and we don't pay one red cent here for rent. In one year the two of us will have so much money we won't know what to do with it!!!

Am I a business man or what??

<u>Levi</u> aching

Yeah..Jayson-you're one hell of a business man!!!

The two of them alternate between the landscaping and trimming of Dr. Duran's estate and the painting of the exterior and interior rooms of the Moreland Motel. As days go by one can see the gradual improvement the motel begins to take on. Levi and Jayson are seen in one the motel room rolling yellow paint up and down on the wall. When Jayson rolls paint up-Levi rolls paint down on the opposite wall. Levi put his hand to his back indicating pain….and gives a slight moan.

Mr. Moreland enters and observes what is taking place. Levi, put your roller down and come here a minute.

Levi complies and immediately inquires of Mr. Moreland-what does he need??

Mr. Moreland

Levi, I want you to take my car to the washer. After you get it cleaned up inside and out…do a nice wax job for me. The wax is in the trunk.

Mr. Moreland gives Levi the keys and Levi disappears-----

Levi at the carwash

Levi is seated in the car as the car-wash process goes into effect. Two car wash slaps soap all over the car as Levi gets into a comfortable sleep-nap position. As the car proceeds through, the spray soap and water, one can readily see Levi is serious about a light snooze. It takes just a little while for the car to go through the rinse then the dry. Two car-dryers are waiting at the end of the car wash.

One of the car washers attempts to get in the car but Levi has unwittingly locked the doors. He tries again to no avail. He looks in and sees a body of a man <u>asleep</u>. The car-washer taps on the glass. No responses. He taps again-then bangs on the door. Levi at this point begins to stir-opens his eyes unlock the doors and achingly drags himself out of the car. He spies a long bench which is a God-send and immediately heads for it. When he gets to it he simply reclines-as he stretches out on the bench he gives off moans of total relief----------

There is hardly any place to wax a car at the Moreland Hotel without the <u>Sun Beaming</u> down on Levi.

He has put a towel over his head and a wide cap on top of the towel.

After dabbing a few spots of wax on the long 1985 Oldsmobile, Levi begins smoothing and waxing in a circular motion----------------------

10 Months Later

It's been more than 3 months since Jayson and Levi have left the hospital. It's Monday morning and the alarm clock goes off at 5 a.m. It is time for the two of them to rise and to make it to Dr. Duran's estate where their daily work schedule awaits them.

The alarm steadily rings as Levi snores away in his bed. Jayson stirs and hollers over to Levi--- Levi!! It's time for us (yawning) to.. to….to work!

Jayson drifts off to sleep in the midst of Levi's snoring. The alarm just keeps on ringing-----------------

Trevor Burlingame arrives in the A.M. hours.

The snoring of Levi and Jayson can be heard from the inside to anyone on the outside. A <u>taxicab</u> pulls up to the door of the two snoozers. The rear door of the taxi opens and out steps a very tall, stately well figured of a woman into the darkness. She steps to the door and knocks furiously. There is no response as the snoring (which continues to be heard from the inside to the outside)...continues...

She knocks and knocks-then she begins to scream through the door.

Levi!! Levi!! I know you're in there. Open the door. (Banging and screaming) Inside Jayson stirs and hollers over to Levi's bed, which is right across from his bed. Levi-a woman's screaming for you-Levi turns-moans and snores once again--------------

Jayson in disgust. Jumps out of the bed.

The door opens to the chain. Jayson inquires.

Who is it?

Is my husband Levi here? I'm Mrs. Burlingame.

The door unlatches as Trevor Burlingame enters. A dim light comes on as the two parties—meet face to face. Jayson looks at Trevor then extends his arm and points toward Levi's bed. She sees him lying on his back steadily snoring. She immediately runs over to him. She falls upon him screaming.

I'm sorry Levi-I'm so sorry-I'm sorry for everything!

As Jayson stands with a look of total surprise Levi awakens and is so overtaken by Trevor's presence he just reaches for her in a warm embrace---

Trevor-Trevor my darling oh how I've missed you.

Jayson (somewhat angry)

Is this the same woman who didn't come to visit you in the hospital??

Levi waves Jayson to be calm..as he kisses and hugs Trevor. Hush Jayson-this is my wife Trevor.

I shore have missed you honey. Kisses between them.

Trevor

Where in the world…I mean where did you go after you left the hospital- (turning to Jayson)….And who in the world is this???

Levi

This is my friend, Jayson. If it had not been for Jayson I'd be dead. (Jayson lashing out at Trevor)

Why didn't you come to the hospital to see about your husband???

You love him <u>sooooo</u> much you didn't even come to see him- when he was near death!

Jayson continues-stepping closer to Trevor who is lying in Levi's arms.

What kind of Lady are you!!!? 12 days without a visit-12 sick days. Not one single phone call!!!! Jayson moves to put on more clothes. Trevor turns to Levi-

I feel real bad about not checking on you Levi-but I was so mad… we lost all that we had….and I blamed you.

Levi (condescending)

Don't worry Trevor honey It'll be fine. I'm just so glad you're here----

(Angrily) I have never seen anything as <u>stupid</u> as all this!!

<u>Levi</u> (Loudly)

Jayson-be quiet!!!!

Jayson finished dressing and grabs up some cover and a pillow then heads toward the door- What kinda love is this--??

If I had a girl who left me for <u>dead</u> she wouldn't <u>be</u> my girl—I'm out of here!

Jayson with the bedding grabs opens the door, steps out and slams the door behind him leaving Levi and Trevor to themselves.

Jayson comes out into the darkness and heads directly to the adjoining building where he and Levi have been painting-he enters the room where it has partially been painted. A bed and mattress are present. He clicks on a light, proceeds to throw on sheets and blankets-Jayson climbs in with his pillow after he clicks off the light. He curls up in his newly acquired bed and makes one last comment.

The craziest-the craziest thing I've ever seen---------- He soon drifts off to sleep--------

As Time passes:

Days go by while Levi, Jayson and <u>Now</u> Trevor who had joined the paint team work diligently painting walls.

Trevor has lost her dress and has dawned pants, boots, and a wide brim work hat. She does mopping and decorating the rooms.

She seems quite content (in spite of the work) being back with her husband.

Jayson takes a moment out just to take a look at Levi and Trevor. His attitude is one of total disgust-he simply shakes his head.

Mr. Moreland enters one of the many rooms that are completed carrying a bucket of paint in each hand. He places the 2 cans of paint on the floor-takes a look at Jayson, Levi and Trevor.

(Excited) You guys are terrific!! We've come a long way. What a team! What a team!!

Interview of Craig Miller-on T.V.

Adrian Vance a Black-African American reporter from station
WTTO interviews the new vice president- Craig
   Miller of Auturo-Engineering and Construction right outside the
Architectural Structure.
   I'm Adrian Vance of WTTO News here with the new vice-
president of Auturo-Engineering and Construction, Mr. Craig
Miller. Mr. Miller! You are the newly appointed vice-president of
Auturo-Engineering.

Craig Miller (speaking through the micro)

Well, for as long as it lasted. Which was 3 months. (Adrian
continues with her questions)
   Tell us Mr. Miller-what really took place with your hue company
and your president's mansion. My viewer's would certainly like to
know.

Mr. Miller (with energy)

They would like to know? I would like to know more than them!
I lost a million dollar salary! It was as though all the internal organs
of the company shut down!! Like in a human body-the kidneys, your
lungs then your heart. BAM it's over--!!
   Now about the president's mansion. Now you see it-pooph-now
you don't. But I've got my suspicions and if I could prove any of it…
They'd have to cart me off to jail.

At the Rancho Love Club there is an African American country singer by the name of Country Nate Green who has been on the rise. He and his country Nate Green singers are performing their award winning country song, <u>Hall of Fame for Lovers</u>. The audience is responding with whistling and applause. They are well into the Country groove of the song, which has already won an ward from Nashville. Country Nate projects the rhythmic message of his original song professionally and receives much more whistling and applause from the audience.

Country Nate gives thank yous and starts on another original country ballad-<u>I put you on a pedestal</u>. Midway through the song one can see Shays Barker at the bar—

Hit me with another one. (Irritated) Bartender I said hit, hit me with another one.

<u>Bartender-Clyde</u>-coming to Shays

We want to thank you for your services but I think you've had enough!

Shays has been drinking shots of alcohol and chasing it with beer—Shays become more irritated at Clyde's refusal. Give me another round man.

<u>Clyde</u>

You've had quite enough and I'm not going to lose my license over you.

I want one more –one more. (Shays pushes up and leans toward the bartender). Clyde reaches for his bat from underneath the bar and proceeds to gently press Shays back down in his seat. Clyde beckons for his 2 security guards to escort Shays out the door, which they do rather roughly--------

Shays protests vehemently making a scene in the process but outside, he goes anyway. Shays apartment-next day

Shays Nightmares

The night finds Shays sleeping… then tossing… then screaming as he awakens from another one of his nightmares, there is sweat streaming from his brow heavy choking of breathing and a look of total fear.

He stumbles from his bed rushes to his bathroom, turns the faucet on, rinses his face, grabs a towel and dries his face. Still at the face bowl he leans over it and looks at himself in the mirror-bows his head and says "God, when will this end!!!" He pauses momentarily then turns and leaves the bathroom and goes into a small room where there is a piano. He seats himself and slowly fingers a melody and starts playing a Beautiful Song. Shays plays a part of the song then slams the piano shut. He simply sits at the piano with his head bowed. Shays sleeps off his drunken spree well into the early afternoon.

After awakening-he cleans himself up and goes back to the side of his bed. He starts remembering the beginning of these problems (a montage) of reflection. His head is bowed and he finally comes to a major decision. Shays jumps up steps to the phone-then-dials-Hello! This is the police? Give me the Captain-yes I said the captain. My name is Shays Barker-I wanna… I wanna make a confession----------

Shay's confession to Levi and Trevor Burlingame

I don't know how to say this other than just to say I'm sorry. I'm sorry about the whole sordid mess! Somehow I just snapped when I was turned down for the 3rd time. Levi just had to give the Vice Presidency to somebody else. My hopes were so high..very high and I had worked so hard for so many years.

I felt there was nothing left for me to do but take from him. To take and take until he had nothing left. I'm truly sorry about hurting Mrs. Burlingame (turning to Trevor). I didn't intend any pain on you. I knew I couldn't hurt Levi without hurting you but I was left with no choice!!!

I'm confessing to you Levi that I tore down that $15,000,000 mansion of yours. I took your furniture, all of your wardrobes, paintings and jewelry. I'm the scoundrel who took it all. All of it Levi.

Mrs. Burlingame cries aloud as Levi looks sternly at Shays in total disbelief.

Shays Confession Continues

Since I'm going through this confession thang I might as well tell the whole story.

I transferred all your available monies and assets to your lowest paid employees. (At this point Levi rises from his seat.)

I called it employee profit sharing Levi; thousands of dollars went to each low paid employee. Banks transferred money to very needy organizations until there were no more funds left. All done in a matter of minutes…by computer.

Levi after taking this all in still stands but tucks his arms to his side and buries his face in his balled fists. Jayson stands by his side with his hand on Levi's shoulder showing full support.

Shays Ending his confession

There is however, a ray of hope-I did <u>not</u> destroy any of the contents of the mansion.

<u>Trevor yells</u> out-

Ooh thank you Lord-thank you.

Shays continue to explain his moves. All of the furniture-wardrobe-expensive paintings and yes the jewelry have been secured in a special location. Even your Rose Royce!!

I'm going to give all of these things back to you Levi..and Mrs. Burlingame. Jayson speaks directly to Levi-

Levi-Levi did ja' hear you and Mrs. Burlingame are getting some of your stuff back!!!

<u>Shays</u>

I will take you and the authorities to where your assets are!!

You're probably wondering why I'm coming forward like I am-

A man has to be able to live with himself. Every since the day the last brick was torn from Levi's mansion I have not had a decent night's sleep. My physical being this past year has gone from serious stomach problems to nightmares to finding no peace of mind at all.

I once was a calm and collected type of man..but now…I'm erratic and extremely nervous. I know with this kind of stress this is the way people develop ulcers and have heart attacks.

Whoever said when your mind is free from worry and you keep good health you have a treasure just with that!! I have always been a decent sort of man…I would like to get back to the man I was!!

Helicopters circle around a remote strip of land that is off the main highway. This strip of land is so remote and so distant that foot-travel is very unlikely.

Word has already spread of the very dramatic <u>confession</u> of <u>Shays Barker</u>-the man responsible for the disappearance or rather the destruction of Levi Burlingame's mansion.

Police cars-newspapers and television cameras are into the moving flow to the designated area left by Shays Barker in the lead police car.

A host of security cars, televisions, cameras, and vans make their way through desolate land-up and down winding seemingly unused roads. Trevor, Levi and Jayson can be seen following the lead car-not enjoying the bumpy and awkwardly wheeling of the officer who is driving.

After miles of traveling this host of cars or if one prefers-this caravan of cars and vans comes to an abrupt halt. All sources remove themselves from their vehicles and stand with a staring blank expression on their faces as if to say (where in the hell are we?)

Shays without hesitation proceeds across the road to a huge row of bushes and vines. He works feverishly to remove the brushes. Moments pass as he pulls and jerks to free the vines from a fence and gate that is hidden behind the brushes.

Once the <u>removal</u> of vines and brushes is complete Shays reaches up to unlock a huge lock. He attempts to push the gate open but the gate seems wedged and doesn't move. Police officers, reporters all join in to push open this wide gate. When it was opened with heavy pressure from all of them, everybody rushed in only to see a clearing for miles around.

The newspaper and television people are taken somewhat by surprise by there being <u>no evidence</u> of anything. Amongst them there were words like-did he lie?? Is this just a publicity stunt?? A female t.v. reporter places a microphone in Shays face.

I'm <u>Colleen Emerson</u> of station A.S.T.B. Television. Mr. Shays, my television viewers have tuned in by the thousands, to see this revelation of yours. There will be no giving back of the $15,000,000 mansion.

But do you intend to give back the wardrobes, expensive paintings, and jewelry? Just what is your assessment??

Heading Directly To Levi Burlingame's Asset.

Police officers & detectives look attentively at Shays as though they have been duped. Shays is facing many years in the penitentiary and many more if he does not produce the Burlingame's assets.

Shays moves quickly away from reporter Emerson and without a word steps over to a small embankment. More grass and vines cover a panel. This panel of buttons and a hand unit that also has 3 switches.

After he removes the vines and grass away from the once hidden panel Shays clicks then clicks, pauses, then click-click. He operates the hand unit and clicks like working a combination to a safe. Even though someone could have accidentally discovered the panel, he would not have the right clicks.

The <u>ground begins to open up</u>. There is a rising door big enough for 2 trucks to drive through. Lights start flashing more than ever as photographers take their pictures of an <u>underground outmoded-</u>outdated <u>airplane</u> <u>hangar.</u> The building, repairing and flying of aircraft has long since been closed for well over 20 years.

It took a superior mind to have thought of all the intricate details of this master plan that by all standards sort of staggers the imagination.

Shays moves to a downward slope and continues down in a curving terminal driveway. Security holds back the masses of the crowd which happened at this time to be enormous & boisterous. Yells and screams of excitement with lights from the t.v. cameras are the order of the day.

The curving terminal moves to a lower level. Lighting comes from a makeshift electrical set-up that Shays has rigged up in the huge underground terminal. From the opening everyone has gone about two hundred feet underground and levels off to where one can see through the dimly lit area a small fleet of trucks. The same trucks that removed the interior possessions and (if I may be so bold) which were skillfully-surgically dismantled from Mr. and Mrs. Burlingame's $15,100,000 mansion. The same trucks that passed through their security gates.

Captain Blanders who is in charge of several squads of policemen, upon spying the trucks, signals to each squad to investigate each truck. Each squad scatters to their assigned truck.

Levi, Trevor, the 2 detectives, Captain Blanders, t.v. personalities, newspapers correspondents, and other dignitary's follow Shays Barker over to a special set-up across from the fleet of trucks.

On a glass table stretching about 4 feet long there are a number of satin jewelry cases. Encased in these satin cases are diamond rings, pearl necklaces, gold bracelets inset with rubies, a number of Rolex watches. Trevor upon taking a closer look at this awesome and very well displayed jewelry setting-screams-my jewelry!!!! My jewelry!!! Levi this is my jewelry!!!

There is more than $350,000 worth of jewelry on the display table. Inspection of the jewelry is made by a detective and Gemologist with their eye-pieces.

Shays pulls a couple of extremely long clothing racks to the forefront. He unzips the long zippers on both racks. The first rack is open and exposes a rack full of mink coats, designer coats, and expensive jackets— Moments pass:

Trevor is so happy and elated, with tears in her eyes she is mulling over her jewelry although security will not let her take them.

The second rack <u>angled away</u> from Trevor consist of gowns, dresses, ladies and men suits and shoes, that could be bought from only the most exclusive of stores.

Levi ambles his way over to the second rack. He sees his fabulous wardrobe-shoes and Trevor's mink coats. He yells for Trevor to join him.

Jayson rushes over to Levi.

<u>Jayson</u>-excited

Man look at those threads! Trevor rushes over to Levi and sees her beautiful minks and gowns. Once again overtaken by surprise she screams and runs to her mink and embraces her wardrobe.

The officers from Captain Blanders squad after moments of checking the trucks bring to him the most artistic paintings. There are twelve paintings in all as Levi who is checking out his suits and shoes turns as he hears reporter Colleen Emerson of A.S.T.B. reporting on air. Many lights are fixated on her.

...And I say to my viewers fabulous sums of jewelry, mink coats stunning wardrobe of evening gowns-designer dresses and shoes-men suits, yes ladies and gentlemen-12 artistic paintings.... valued into the hundreds of thousands of dollars.

Levi at witnessing the exposure of his very special paintings, just smiles and shakes his head-swings his arms and hollers in complete jubilation.

Yes!! Yes!! I got my paintings back yes-yes...ohh Thank God!!!

Trucks are maneuvered into various positions as security removes the items <u>aboard</u> modern refrigerators- freezers-stoves-china closets-beds-televisions-tables and chairs are all removed.

When all of the trucks are emptied, it looks like a storage house for furniture rather than an old <u>hangar for</u> <u>building</u> and <u>repairing</u> <u>airplanes.</u>

Trevor is just <u>ecstatic</u> over the <u>return of all of her interior</u> <u>possessions.</u>

Shays has done a remarkable job of securing and maintaining every single item. Levi and Trevor Burlingame are truly blessed to be as fortunate as to regain their very expensive interior possessions.

Now on T.V. more than a multitude of people have come to see the culmination of answers to the disappearance of the $15,000,000 mansion.

Television continues to attract people and show the <u>underground hangar</u>. From inside with some darkness but lighting from the T.V. cameras provide more light as the cameras exposed the items. Levi overtaken with joy goes to Trevor and takes her hands. With tears of happiness she is led to Captain Blanders. Cameras fall upon the three of them as Levi speaks.

Captain-we have all our possessions back! <u>We don't want to press any formal charges against Shays Barker-No</u> chargers at all!!

People are stunned at these remarks coming from Levi. Captain Blanders speaks to the both of them. Mr. and Mrs. Burlingame this man has committed an atrocious act. Look around you. See what he has taken from the privacy of your home. Trevor intervenes. Yes what you say is true-but we have it all back now, Thank God!

Captain Blanders continues with his quest to see Shays pay for what he perceives as a criminal act. One that requires going to prison.

What about your $15,000,000 mansion Mr. and Mrs. Burlingame? Do you wish to just let that fabulously beautiful home go as well??

Trevor (intervenes once again)

Yes! We can build another home. Shays was our number one construction engineer. We did not treat him right. We know why he did what he did------!!!

Levi (directly to the captain)

Captain Blanders there is to be no penalty imposed upon Shays Barker. We have signed no formal charges against him. Just let him go!!

More ooohhhhhs and aahhs come from the crowd as reporter Emerson has held the microphone close enough to pick up the conversation as the cameras were rolling.

As Levi and Mrs. Burlingame impress upon Captain Blanders the importance and urgency to drop all charges against Shays Barker, one of the female security officers screeches up to them in a highly polished late model Rose Royce.

<u>Jayson</u> (screams out seeing the Rose)

Oh-now that's what I'm talking about-The captain appears to have no other choice than to signal two men from his squad to escort Shays top-side.

<u>Captain Blanders</u>

Don't worry Mr. and Mrs. Burlingame we'll take care of things here- (Blanders open the door for Trevor as Mr. Levi Burlingame's steps into the drivers seat and Jayson springs into the back-seat)

We'll just sign you off on this Rose---

Topside the cameras make their way to Shays and he asked one question by Reporter Emerson- Do you have any comments Mr. Barker, anything you wish to say??

I gave back to Mr. and Mrs. Burlingame what I could. I am sorry. But now I can look at myself in the mirror and see my old-self again------

Shays pulls away in the opposite direction and heads through the crowd. He eventually clears the crowd and walks over a wide old landing strip. He continues to walk alone as the Rose Royce driven by Levi Burlingame proceeds to the top level. Levi watches Shays as he can barely be seen moving…moving..directly to who knows where.

The Rose slowly makes it through the crowd (with lights flashing) to the road then accelerating-----

Shays walked away, a free man.

WASH ME THOROUGHLY FROM MINE INIQUITY,
AND CLEANSE ME FROM MY SIN.

PSALMS 51:2

CREATE IN ME A CLEAN HEART, O GOD; AND
RENEW A RIGHT SPIRIT WITHIN ME.

PSALMS 51:10

Country Nate Green
(662) 627-3140